ELKO
LORD OF THE SEA

BY ADAM BLADE

ORCHARD

THE NEW AGE

ELKO
LORD OF THE SEA

With special thanks to Michael Ford

To George Bolton, a great friend

www.beastquest.co.uk

ORCHARD BOOKS
338 Euston Road, London NW1 3BH
Orchard Books Australia
Level 17/207 Kent St, Sydney, NSW 2000

A Paperback Original
First published in Great Britain in 2012

Beast Quest is a registered trademark of Beast Quest Limited
Series created by Beast Quest Limited, London

Text © Beast Quest Limited 2012
Cover and inside illustrations by Steve Sims © Orchard Books 2012

A CIP catalogue record for this book is available from
the British Library.

ISBN 978 1 40831 841 6

3 5 7 9 10 8 6 4 2

Printed and bound by CPI Group (UK) Ltd, Coydon, CR0 4YY

The paper and board used in this paperback are natural recyclable
products made from wood grown in sustainable forests. The
manufacturing processes conform to the environmental regulations of
the country of origin.

Orchard Books is a division of Hachette Children's Books,
an Hachette UK company

www.hachette.co.uk

I heard of Avantia in my youth, when I flew with the other children over the plains of Henkrall. They said it was a land of beauty, bravery and honour. A place of noble Beasts, too.

Even then it made me sick.

I can't fly now. My cruel mistress, Kensa, was jealous of my wings, so she took them. Don't pity me, Avantians – it's you who should be afraid. Your time is coming. Kensa has plans for your green and pleasant land. Your Good Beasts will be no defence against her servants – they'll be powerless!

You'll need more than courage to protect you from the Beasts of Henkrall!

Your sworn enemy,

Igor

PROLOGUE

Kensa leant across the table until her chin was level with the rough wooden boards.

The Sorceress stared at the six clay figurines lined up in a row and her eyes gleamed with wicked delight. "How are you, my pretties?" she hissed.

Finally, the figures were ready! She hadn't slept for days, spending all her time in her workshop, frantically crafting each of them from the earth of Henkrall. Now it was almost time to unleash them.

"First you will conquer this kingdom," she whispered. "And then – Avantia!"

Kensa threw back her head and cackled. Her laughter echoed off the vaulted stone ceiling above. From the far side of the chamber, her one-eyed servant, Igor, laughed too. In the shadows, his hunchbacked figure shifted and his chains rattled.

"Did I say you could join in?" snapped Kensa.

Igor's laughter died. He scratched at his wrists where the manacles dug into his skin. "Sorry, Mistress," he muttered.

Kensa thought about loosening her slave's bonds – it wasn't as if he ever tried to escape. *No, let him suffer.*

And soon others would join him in
suffering. Whole kingdoms would
crawl to her feet and beg for mercy.

She returned her gaze to the
figurines and imagined seeing their
terrible shapes in giant form. Six new
Beasts to wreak havoc, to trample,
burn and tear apart lands. *And all*

at my will! Kensa rubbed her hands together with glee.

"Just one more ingredient needed," she said.

She stood up, wrapping her leather robe around herself, and marched towards the large chest in the corner of the chamber. Lights from candles caught the designs on her robe – gold and silver threads spelling out strange curled symbols. "I need power and strength for my creations," she said. "I need the blood of six Good Beasts. And I know exactly how to get it!"

She kicked the lid of the chest open and reached inside, taking out a long, metal staff carved with intricate spirals and swirls. Igor cowered further into his corner. His single eye blinked in fear.

"It's all right," said Kensa, grinning.

"This isn't to beat you with."

She strode across to the window, which looked out over Henkrall from the top of her mountain castle. Thin grey clouds were deepening to a bruised purple shade. Thunder rolled like the pounding of distant hooves.

Perfect. A storm is just what I need…

"I'll be going on a little trip," she said. "To Avantia."

Igor's head jerked up. "Avantia? I've heard it's a land full of brave heroes who fight evil."

"One less hero now," Kensa sneered. "Haven't you heard? Taladon, Master of the Beasts, has perished at last."

Kensa stepped onto the window ledge, feeling the bitter wind of Henkrall whip around her body. Lights flashed in the storm clouds

and the rain fell like iron daggers.
The Sorceress of Henkrall felt
electricity in the air and the staff in
her hand tingled. The ancient magic
was building – the forbidden power to
travel between kingdoms. With a last

glance at her six Evil Beast models, she lifted the metal staff above her head and waited for the lightning to strike.

CHAPTER ONE

A FINAL PARTING

The Golden Armour had never felt so heavy.

Tom's shoulders sagged beneath the weight of the metal pieces, and the driving rain rattled off the breastplate like a thousand hurled stones. Under the lead-grey sky, the gold had no gleam.

Before him stood an ornate wagon pulled by two horses in ceremonial tassels. The clouds had opened just as the funeral ended and Taladon's coffin was being loaded inside. Now, most of the mourners had left the Palace Garden to return to their duties. Tom stood with Elenna and his mother, Freya, on either side of him. King Hugo had remained as well, wearing his ceremonial armour. Aduro waited with them, his waterlogged robe dragging in the dirt.

On Tom's arm, his shield hummed, sending vibrations up to his shoulder. The tokens of the Six Good Beasts were flowing with their grief, and it only added to Tom's misery.

Elenna put a hand on his shoulder. "The Armour suits you," she said, with a sad smile.

Tom tried to smile back, but couldn't. He'd worn the Armour

before he'd learned his father was still alive. And since that time, he'd dreamed of wearing it again. But he'd always known that could never happen while Taladon was Master of the Beasts. Now it felt like a weight he could hardly bear.

"I miss him," said Tom.

Elenna nodded.

She's lost both her parents, thought Tom. *She knows how it feels.*

Freya stepped forward and held out a sword and scabbard in both hands. "We all miss Taladon," she said. "But we must be strong. Here – a warrior takes his sword with him."

Tom understood. He took the sword, walked slowly to the wagon, and placed the sheathed blade on top of the coffin.

"Bear him carefully to the Tombs,"

said King Hugo to the driver. The
King's voice cracked. Taladon and
Hugo had been friends since before
Tom was born.

The wagon creaked off as the horses
plodded over the soggy ground, their
heads bobbing. Tom watched it move
slowly towards the city gates. From
there it would travel to the Gallery
of Tombs, the resting place of every
Master of the Beasts since the first,
Tanner.

One day, a tomb will be opened for me, too, thought Tom.

He felt a hand slide onto his shoulder and squeeze. Freya was staring intently at him.

"I have to go now," she said. "Gwildor needs me."

Tom nodded – he'd always known his mother would one day return to her duties as Gwildor's Mistress of the Beasts. They embraced, and as he looked over Freya's shoulder, he saw that Aduro had already conjured a portal to take her home. It shimmered in the air like a mirage.

Freya pulled away from him. "You're the Master of the Beasts now," she said. "I know you'll make me proud."

With two steps she reached the portal. With the third she was gone.

The blurred air stilled once more.

For years Tom had believed both his parents were dead. Then, through many Quests, he'd found them both again, and discovered each was a brave warrior sworn to defend their kingdoms. Now one was lost forever, and the other would be risking her life far away.

Tom had never felt so alone.

King Hugo stepped towards him. Rain streaked down his face and beard.

"Your father was the bravest man I ever met," he said. "Avantia owes him a debt that cannot be measured in gold or precious stones."

The King's words stirred the embers of Tom's pride, and he found himself standing straighter beneath the heavy armour.

"I mean to carry on his duties with honour and courage," he said. "I'm ready to take on a new Quest."

Aduro gave a thin smile.

"Of course you want to take your mind off things," he said, "but there are no Quests to undertake. Malvel is dead, his evil scoured from the kingdom. Why don't you enjoy a well-earned—"

A scream of creaking wood interrupted the Wizard's words and Tom felt a pain lance up his arm.

"Tom!" gasped Elenna. "Your shield!"

Tom held the shield close to his chest and looked at the surface. Epos's talon was glowing scarlet, pulling against the rain-soaked wood with a grinding sound as if trying to break free.

"The Flame Bird must be in danger!" said Tom.

Aduro quickly touched two fingers to the talon and his lips moved in a silent spell. Red light burst from the shield, forming into an orb as tall as Tom. In the midst of the sphere an image appeared. Tom, Elenna and their companions stared.

"Stonewin!" Elenna gasped.

Tom made out the shape of the volcano's black, lava-scarred slopes, wreathed in thick cloud. As they watched, a dark shape burst through the cloud. Tom recognised the red-brown feathers and golden beak of Epos the Flame Bird. But on the Beast's back knelt a tall woman with gleaming red hair. She wore a black leather cloak, patched together with steel clasps and pins, which fluttered in the wind. Dozens of metal bracelets dangled from her wrists and jewelled rings glittered on her fingers.

"Who is that?" asked Tom.

Aduro's face was pale. He stepped forward towards the image, hands shaking. "It can't be…" he muttered.

The woman clutched a long metal staff in one hand, but in the other she held a dagger with a strange curved

blade. Lifting it above her head, she plunged it into Epos's back. The Flame Bird screeched so loudly Tom's knees felt weak and he had to clamp shut his eyes.

"No!" he cried.

When he could open his eyes to see again, the good Beast was veering wildly in the sky as the evil rider drew out the blade. With perfect balance, she held a vial in her other hand, and let drops of blood drip into the open mouth. She slipped the vial into her robe. Then, grinning wickedly, she tipped sideways, somersaulting off the Flame Bird's back and landing on the mountain slope.

Epos swooped away, screeching wildly, but seemingly unhurt. The woman slipped the dagger into a scabbard at her waist, then lifted the metal staff towards the sky. Tom saw her green eyes glint with malice.

"What's she doing?" muttered Elenna.

Lightning forked above Stonewin, and for a fraction of a heartbeat Tom saw it strike the staff. The image of the metal rod, sizzling with pure white light, was etched into his brain. When the brightness died, the woman had gone. Only a few tendrils of spiralling smoke remained.

The red orb shrank and died away, leaving them all watching the driving rain.

CHAPTER TWO

SORCERESS OF HENKRALL

King Hugo spoke first. "Is that woman dead?" he asked.

Aduro shook his head. "If that's who I think it is, *we* might all be dead soon."

Tom's heart beat faster, a mixture of excitement and fear chasing away the remains of his grief. *I wanted a Quest*, he thought, *and it looks like I've found one.*

"Who is she?" asked Elenna.

Aduro looked at each of them in turn, his face grey and grave. "That was Kensa," he said. "A foe I never thought I'd lay eyes on again. She plies her evil ways in a mysterious kingdom called Henkrall."

"I've never heard of it," said King Hugo.

"There is no reason why you should," said Aduro. "It's forbidden to travel between Avantia and Henkrall. And almost impossible."

"Almost?" said Tom.

Aduro nodded. "Kensa was banished there long ago. She sought great power – an elemental, ancient kind of magic forbidden by the Circle of Wizards."

Tom was growing impatient. "But what was she doing to Epos with that dagger?" he asked. "It felt like the talon would explode from my shield at any moment."

"I don't know," said Aduro. "Have you felt anything else strange?"

"My shield's been humming with energy all morning," said Tom. "The Beasts are grieving…" His stomach twisted with dread. "Perhaps it wasn't grief at all. Maybe it was pain. What if Kensa's attacked the other Beasts too?"

Aduro's wrinkled hands clenched into fists. "It's my fault!" he said. "I should have sensed an enemy was near!"

Elenna placed a hand on the Wizard's arm. "You've just lost a close friend," she said.

"None of us are ourselves today," added King Hugo.

The humming in Tom's shield had stopped, so perhaps the Beasts were safe again. *But I have to know what happened in that vision.* He reached down to his belt and took out the ruby jewel, won from his battle with Torgor the Minotaur.

"What are you doing?" asked King Hugo.

"The ruby lets me hear the thoughts of Beasts," said Tom. "I want to see if it works from a distance too."

He held the ruby against the Flame Bird's talon on his shield.

"Good thinking!" said Aduro. "Can you sense anything?"

Tom closed his eyes, concentrating on picking up Epos's thoughts. They drifted into focus like a half-forgotten memory.

"She's thinking about a 'strange

woman'…" Tom muttered.

"That must be Kensa," said Elenna.

The voice was weak in Tom's head, but he heard a phrase repeated over and over. Slowly he made it out: *Stealing…blood.*

He lost Epos's voice in the pounding rain.

"She's stealing blood," he said. "It must be for some terrible magic she's working on."

"Then there's only one thing to do," said Tom. "We have to go to Henkrall and stop her carrying out her plans, whatever they are."

"No," said Aduro. "You cannot get to Henkrall."

"But Kensa travelled there," Tom said.

"What I mean," said Aduro, "is that the use of such magic is too dangerous. And it is forbidden."

Tom's frustration flared. "I won't stand by, however dangerous or forbidden it is."

Aduro was silent for a long time. "Very well," said the Wizard at last, "but you must know: I cannot accompany you. My magic isn't strong enough. You will have to travel by the Lightning Path. It's extremely perilous, so fraught with danger that the Circle of Wizards banned it hundreds of years ago. Many sorcerers died attempting it."

Sheet lightning flashed above in the clouds, followed by a growl of thunder. Tom shivered.

King Hugo faced Aduro. "Are you sure you want to do this?" he asked.

Why's he asking Aduro? Tom wondered. *It's my Quest...*

His old friend nodded slowly.

"And you?" asked the King, turning to Tom. "No one will think any the less of you if you decline."

Tom looked at Elenna, whose eyes shone with determination.

"No one should be able to harm the Good Beasts of Avantia and get away with it," he said. "My father lived by that rule, and so shall I. We'll travel the Lightning Path."

"Very well," said Aduro. "May fate look kindly upon you both."

Elenna's face broke into a grin. "I'll fetch Storm and Silver from the stables," she said.

"No," said Tom. "We can't risk them on the Lightning Path. We travel alone."

Elenna nodded. "You're right. How do we use this Path?"

Aduro pointed back towards the Palace. "Follow me."

They set off towards the main buildings of the Palace complex, but Aduro stopped. "I almost forgot!" he said. With a click of his fingers, the Golden Armour vanished from Tom's body. "It's safely back in the Armoury," said Aduro.

Though he was not wearing the

Armour any more, Tom knew he still enjoyed the magical properties it possessed. *I'll need all the strength of heart from the golden breastplate on this Quest*, he thought.

They climbed the steps to Aduro's chamber. The Wizard went to a wooden cabinet on the wall. A key appeared in his hand and he unlocked the door. Inside, fastened to the wall, was a long silver staff, just like the one that they'd seen Kensa use. As the Wizard handed it over, Tom noticed his hand was shaking.

"The power of the staff should not be underestimated," he said.

He withdrew a leather pouch from the cabinet and tossed it to Elenna. She opened it and poured a handful of silver coins into her palm. Tom saw

a motif of two wings etched into the surface.

"This is the currency of Henkrall," said Aduro. "In case you need to buy provisions."

"What now?" asked Tom.

Aduro's eyes filled with fear. "Now you go outside and…wait to be hit by lightning."

CHAPTER THREE

A NEW KINGDOM

They stood on the tallest of King Hugo's walls, while the storm crashed around them. Tom's clothes were soaked to his skin, and Elenna's hair hung in damp trails over her face. Aduro was beside them, his robes whipped by the wind.

"Are you sure?" he asked. "No one can force you to take this risk."

Despite the cold, the staff felt warm

in Tom's hand. Lightning flashed in the clouds and thunder shook. The storm was right above them.

"I'm ready," he said, lifting the staff skywards. Elenna clutched his arm.

"Farewell," said Aduro, his expression etched with terror.

The staff hummed with energy, making the hairs on Tom's body stand on end. Then lightning forked, burning itself into his eyelids. The staff sizzled, hot in his hand, and power greater than any he had felt before ripped through his body.

Tom felt Elenna's fingers digging into his arm. He opened his eyes slowly, expecting blinding light. But instead he saw a blue sky and green fields. Was this Henkrall? His hand grasped thin air – the staff had disappeared!

Tom swivelled round, speechless. They were standing on the edge of a cliff. Behind them, a barren valley stretched towards mountains.

"It worked!" gasped Elenna.

Tom turned to his friend and chuckled. Her hair was standing up straight, and however hard she tried to smooth it down it sprang back up.

"Not funny!" she said, but a smile played over her lips too.

Tom realised it was the first time they'd laughed together since his father's death. He noticed his sword lying on the ground nearby. It must have fallen out of his scabbard. As he reached to pick it up, his hand jolted back. He cried out as the blade fizzed and crackled with blue light. Now Elenna was laughing harder. Tom reached out again. This time it was fine, and he sheathed the blade at his side. As he did, he saw Elenna's smile had slipped away.

"Tom, your shield…"

He pulled it round to face him, and dropped it in shock. The tokens were missing. "No…" he muttered, searching the ground around them. "How?"

He'd won each token on his first six

Quests. The Good Beasts of Avantia, freed from Malvel's evil, had given them to him as a symbol of their gratitude. They each empowered him with a magic skill and were his most prized possessions. His panic turned to anger. "It must have something to do with Kensa stealing the Good Beasts' blood," he said.

"We'll get them back," said Elenna. "Don't worry."

Tom checked his belt. At least the jewels remained. And he didn't need to be wearing the Golden Armour to summon its powers. *I'm weaker than normal*, he thought, *but I'm not defenceless*.

What about the Beasts? Without their tokens in his shield, were they vulnerable?

"Tom, look!" said Elenna. She was pointing to the shield on the ground.

In place of the tokens, something

45

else had appeared. Tom knelt down, with Elenna crouching beside him, and picked up the shield. A map had etched itself across the surface, carved into the wood. It showed rivers, towns, hills and valleys.

Tom grinned. "Perhaps Aduro's magic hasn't abandoned us after all."

"Thank you, Aduro!" Elenna called.

She walked to the edge of the cliff top, and Tom joined her. A faint

breeze fluttered their clothes. Looking carefully over the precipice, Tom saw jagged rocks below.

"Henkrall is huge," said Elenna. "We'll need some sort of transport."

"We might be able to climb down from here," Tom said. It would be a start.

He used the power of the golden helmet to peer into the distance. At first he couldn't see any sign of life. *Kensa's out there somewhere*, he thought. Scanning along the rugged cliff-faces, something caught his eye.

Chimneys. Windows. A building. As Tom's eyes adjusted he realised what he was seeing. "A town!" he muttered. It clung to the cliff-face. Sheer drops from the doors of the buildings looked out over nothing. It was as though, at any moment, the whole town could crash into the abyss. But it wasn't deserted.

Tom saw people threading between the streets, and smoke rising from fires.

He described what he was seeing to Elenna, whose normal eyesight wasn't powerful enough to see the town.

"Maybe they'll be able to tell us where Kensa is," said Elenna. "Let's go."

She led the way, picking a route down the cliff-face until they reached a rough sheep track. Then they began to climb back up the other side, following a steep path. As they neared the town, Tom couldn't work out why people would settle in such a place. It was almost impossible to reach by cart or horse. There weren't any roads. Yet the town seemed to be thriving – Tom heard noises from the market and smelled roasting food.

They had to cross a tricky patch of rock, hundreds of feet up. "Be careful," said Elenna, as he walked along the narrow ledge. "And don't look—"

She cried out as her foot slipped. Loose pebbles rained down. Tom, a few paces behind, had no chance of reaching her in time. Elenna fell, her hands scrambling to find a hold. Her body tilted away from the cliff, and her eyes widened with terror. Tom felt his scream lodge in his throat as his friend tumbled into thin air.

He'd been too slow to save her. Elenna was plunging to her death!

CHAPTER FOUR

THE FLYING FOLK OF HENKRALL

Elenna's body rolled over and over as she hurtled towards the ground.

A shape swooped from the shadow of the cliffs below – a huge bird – and gripped Elenna in its talons. Tom gasped, feeling sick, as it climbed back up through the air on powerful wings. But his eyes must have been playing tricks on him. The 'bird' had the head of a person with a mouth and nose and ears, instead of a beak. It had a mop of blond hair instead of feathers. Tom gasped as the creature flew closer. It wasn't clutching Elenna with talons, but arms! What Tom had thought were tail feathers were two human legs.

"It's a…" Words failed him. Tom was looking at a flying man!

The person alighted on a flat shelf of rock, and placed Elenna on her feet. She stared at the man as he furled his wings against his back. "Thank you!" she gasped.

Tom approached slowly.

"What are you?" said the man, frowning.

"We're people of Avantia," Tom replied. "I'm Tom, and this is Elenna."

"I'm Rorden," said the man. "And you're strangers to Henkrall, I think?"

"What makes you say that?" asked Elenna.

The man spread his wings again, and gestured over his shoulder. "Because you haven't got these, of course!"

Elenna shared an astonished look with Tom. "Does everyone have wings in this kingdom?" she asked.

Rorden frowned. "Does no one

have wings where you come from?"

"Only the birds," said Tom.

The man laughed. "Wait 'til I tell me wife about that! Speaking of which, I must be leaving." He leapt off the cliff, spread his wings, and hovered for a moment. "Be careful," he said. "Mind your step!"

He tilted his wings and flapped away.

For a moment, Tom and Elenna stared after him. "Perhaps only Kensa is evil here," said Tom.

"Then we can't let this kingdom suffer," said Elenna.

They pressed on into the town. The buildings seemed to have been carved from the rock face. They had doors, with ledges halfway up their fronts, and Tom and Elenna walked beneath flying people coming and going. Barely anyone paid them any attention, even when they reached the market square. Among the stalls Tom recognised, selling food or pottery, were others that made his mouth drop open. A man with black spiky hair, with gold rings on his fingers, pointed at Tom. "There's a boy who wants a pet, I see!"

"No," said Tom. "We're just—"

"A dog?" said the man. He looked around his feet. "I've got one that can fly and catch at the same time."

"We're looking—"

"Ah, you're a cat man! This one can spot a flying mouse at fifty paces."

"Actually," said Elenna, "we're looking for animals for transport. °Do you sell anything like that?"

The man's smile turned into a frown, and he jerked a thumb sideways. "Two stalls along," he said.

"Old Peter might have something."

Tom thanked him. They found a bearded man picking his teeth with his dirty nails. He eyed them suspiciously as they approached his stall.

"Greetings," said Tom. "We were told you might sell animals for transport."

Old Peter's wings ruffled. "Just two left," he said, nodding at a stable nearby. "Take a look."

Tom and Elenna peered into the stable. A squat horse with a purplish coat was munching on hay. Beside him lay a snoozing wolf, twice Silver's size, with a matted, shaggy black pelt.

"A wolf and a horse," Elenna muttered. "It could be a sign."

Tom reached out to stroke the horse's nose, but it shied away. The wolf yawned lazily. "They're not quite as noble as

Storm and Silver, are they?" said Tom.

He looked back to Old Peter. "Do you have anything else?"

"Tempest and Spark's your lot," said the trader. "Their owners abandoned them because they never grew wings. Three silver pieces and they're yours."

Tempest whinnied and Tom thought of Storm, waiting for him back in

King Hugo's stables. This stallion might not have Storm's courage, but he looked sturdy enough. Elenna crouched beside the wolf and tickled his ears. "Spark, you say?" she said.

Old Peter raised his eyebrows. "You're a natural. That animal nearly took my hand off earlier."

"We'll take them," Tom said.

Elenna paid Old Peter three pieces.

"Good luck with 'em," said the seller, grinning as he pocketed the money. Tom thought he heard him add, "You'll need it!" under his breath.

Tom and Elenna led the animals on a narrow path out of town. Elenna struggled onto Spark's back, gripping two tufts of hair. Tempest didn't have a saddle, which meant Tom had to ride him bareback. He gently nudged

Tempest's flanks to get the horse trotting.

"I've never ridden a wolf before," Elenna said.

"I don't think Silver would let you," Tom joked. He tried to keep Tempest on the path by pulling on his mane. The stallion kept wandering off towards the edge, where tufts of grass sprouted.

When the town had disappeared behind a curve in the cliff, Tom brought Tempest to a halt and looked at his shield. A path was marked in the wood in a glowing line like molten gold. It led right to the heart of the kingdom.

Tempest tossed his head.

"I think I know where we need to head," Tom said.

"To find a Beast?" asked Elenna.

Tempest started to move towards

the edge of the cliff again. *Something's spooked him*, Tom thought. "Whoa, boy!" he muttered, gripping Tempest's mane.

Tempest broke into a canter.

"Tom?" called Elenna, her voice laced with panic.

Tom yanked harder on the horse's mane, but Tempest shook his head. Tom threw his arms around the horse's neck as it careered towards the edge of the cliff. *This horse will kill us both!* He was about to hurl himself clear, when Tempest leapt off.

The ground yawned hundreds of feet below. Tom heard a ripping sound and two wings like lilac sails arced from the stallion's sides. They twitched and fluttered as they caught the wind.

"Amazing!" called Elenna. She swooped beside him on Spark. The wolf had sprouted wings too, black as those of a raven. "We're flying!"

Tom grinned as he gripped the horse's mane. Three silver pieces was a bargain for two flying animals! Did Old Peter realise what these creatures could do?

They steered their animals towards the heart of Henkrall.

CHAPTER FIVE

KENSA'S WORKSHOP

Tom had flown on Beasts before,
but he struggled to control Tempest.
Without a saddle, the ridge of the
horse's spine dug into his backside
and the flying stallion responded
jerkily to the tiniest tugs on his mane.
When Tom nudged his flanks with his
feet, Tempest veered left or right.
His wings heaved through the air.

"I don't think he's used to being

ridden!" Tom called across to Elenna.

But his friend seemed to be having no such problems. She flew straight and true on Spark's back. The wolf's wings were shorter and coated in shaggy black hair.

Soon, though, Tempest had calmed down and Tom was able to control him better. Every so often, they would pass over towns and villages below, with people taking off from the roofs of buildings. They saw a group of children playing a game of aerial catch.

"This place is like nothing I've ever seen!" said Elenna.

Tom couldn't help a smile of wonder spreading over his face as a flock of birds soared right past them. But his smile vanished when his eyes fell on a dark, pine-clad mountain

range ahead. On top of the tallest
peak was what looked like a castle
ruin. "I wonder who lives there?"
he called to Elenna.

Something about the strange

broken battlements drew him in.
He pulled his shield in front of him,
keeping one hand on the horse's
mane. "The castle is right in the
centre of the kingdom," he said.
"There aren't any other settlements
anywhere nearby. This must be where
the map has been leading us."

"Let's go and take a look," Elenna replied.

They steered their animals upwards
and towards the looming mountains.
As they neared the castle, Tom could
see it wasn't built on the peak, but
from it. The jutting fist of rock at
the top of the mountain had been
carved into turrets and walkways,
battlements and windows. The air
became chilly and damp as they
broke through shreds of cloud. Tom
made out faint candlelight flickering
through arched windows and he

heard the clank of metal coming from inside. Smoke trailed into the sky from several chimneys.

It sounds like a forge, he thought, *or some sort of workshop.*

The feeling of unease built as they flew closer, and the hair on Tom's neck stood on end. He hissed to Elenna and pointed to a large open window at one end. Then he put his finger to his lips. *Quiet.*

The animals' wings moved through the air silently. Tom peered through the open window. There were rows of shelves, covered in dusty books and jars of strange liquids. Other glass cases held floating, shapeless creatures. Lanterns hung on the walls casting ghostly shadows.

A piece of machinery, a mixture of steel coils and bubbling pots, vented steam in one corner.

"Out of my way!" snapped a woman's voice. Tom drew back slightly from the window as a cowering, hunchbacked creature retreated across the floor, dragging a set of clanking chains from his ankles and wrists. He only had one eye – the other was swollen shut.

A hooded woman, taller than Taladon had been, strode past the hunchback in a fur-lined cloak that brushed the ground. As the light caught her face, Tom recognised her narrowed green eyes. Kensa! Silver threads in her robe picked out strange symbols and arrows, broken circles and what looked like writing. Kensa was carrying a polished wooden box which she laid on the table. She lowered her hood and shook out her red locks. "It's time, Igor," she said.

He gave a wheezing chuckle and shifted for a better look. Tom grimaced as he saw the creature's back – there were scarred stumps instead of wings, stained with dried blood.

Kensa unlatched the box and opened the lid. Inside were six carved figurines of Beasts Tom had never seen before. Kensa placed each of the figures on the table and then she reached inside her cloak. Glass tinkled as she drew out a chain looped through the stoppers of six glass vials, each filled with scarlet liquid.

"The Beasts' blood!" Elenna whispered.

Kensa opened the first vial and poured a trickle over one of the moulds. It soaked into the clay and Kensa began to chant.

"Blood of Beast and earth of home,
Join to become flesh and bone.
Create new evil, see what spreads:
Six new Beasts for all to dread!"

She repeated the words again and
again as she poured blood over the
little clay statues. A flash filled the
room. Scarlet smoke rose in snaking

tendrils from the figures. Kensa grinned. "Soon my Beasts will rule this kingdom," she said.

"Aren't you afraid, Mistress?" asked Igor. "Don't you fear punishment?"

Kensa's head snapped round. "And who will punish me?" she asked. "That toothless Circle of Wizards? By the time my Beasts have conquered Henkrall, it will be too late. I can't wait to see that old fool Aduro's face when we march into Avantia. It's his fault I'm banished here."

A blast of wind caught Tom and as he clutched the horse's mane tighter, one of Tempest's hooves knocked the window ledge. Kensa and Igor turned towards him.

"Who's there?" asked the hunchback.

Kensa stood bolt upright and her eyes narrowed. "Intruders!"

CHAPTER SIX

SKY BATTLE

"Fly away!" Tom yelled to Elenna.

As their animals shot up and away from the castle wall, a bolt of silver light leapt through the window, just missing Tempest's legs.

"After them!" Kensa screeched.

Tom heard the clang of chains, then scampering feet. A moment later, Igor burst from the window on a flying bristle-backed hog with wild yellow

eyes. He still had a section of his
chain wrapped around his hand.

Tom wheeled his stallion around to
climb further from the castle, but Igor
was quick, darting through the sky
towards them.

Kensa leant from the window.
"It's Taladon's brat!" she shouted.
"Bring me his head, Igor!"

The one-eyed servant snarled in

delight, letting the chain uncoil from his wrist. With a vicious flick of his wrist, it snaked through the air. Tom ducked low against Tempest's back as the whip cut above his head. If it hit him, he'd have no chance.

Tom waited until the next attack, and as the whip sailed past, just a hair's breadth from Tempest's nose, he drew his sword. "Dare to fight me fairly?" he called.

"Why bother?" Igor sneered, unleashing another lash.

Elenna swooped past, gripping Spark's flanks with her knees as she shot an arrow from her bow. It skimmed the hide of Igor's animal.

Their enemy rattled his chain whip. "You two are pathetic! I hope you can fly!"

As Igor drew back his arm, Tom

pressed Tempest's neck. The stallion seemed to understand – he was a quick learner – and dropped swiftly through the air towards Kensa's servant. One swing of Tom's sword severed the chain from the manacle at Igor's wrist. Tom wheeled around on Tempest and brought his blade to Igor's throat. The hunchback's mouth dropped open in astonishment.

"Useless swine!" shouted Kensa, leaning from her window far below.

Igor jerked away and reached into a pouch strapped to the hog's side. Tom caught the glint of spiked balls in his hand. Igor hurled them towards Tom and Elenna.

Tom lifted his shield to protect himself, and felt one ball bounce off the surface. Tempest wasn't quick enough and whinnied in agony as several buried themselves in his side. Spark howled too. Tempest reared and Tom had to cling desperately to his mane. He fought to control the bucking stallion and saw Elenna spinning on Spark's back, his wings flapping madly and blood trailing from his black fur.

Tom managed to steady Tempest, and saw Elenna leaning down to pull the ball from Spark's hind leg.

"Care for some more?" said Igor.

The hunchback hovered above them, grabbing another handful of deadly missiles. *We've no chance in the open*, Tom thought. Glancing around, he saw a bank of thick grey cloud about an arrow's flight away. "Quick!" he shouted to Elenna. "Hide in there!"

Spark jerked through the air

just as another hail of spiked balls
whizzed down. Tom guided Tempest
at galloping speed into the cloud.
As soon as they entered the foggy
path, Tom could barely see five paces
ahead. He flew on blindly, hearing
Spark's panting breath right behind
him. There was no other way to
lose Igor.

"I can't see them!" called the hunchback.

"Well, find them, you oaf!" Kensa screamed from the castle.

As Tom and Elenna flew through the cloud, their clothes became heavy with damp. They heard the flap of the hog's stubby wings – close then distant, then close again – as Igor scoured the dense fog. Tom could smell rotten breath, and wondered whether it was the hog's, or Igor's. Eventually, the sound vanished.

"He's given up," Elenna whispered. Her hair hung in wet trails from the cloud's moisture.

Slowly, they guided their animals out of the clouds. Kensa's castle loomed some distance away, so they alighted on a rocky plateau, out of sight.

"I can't believe we ran away!" said Tom.

"We had no choice," said Elenna. "This is a new kingdom, with a new way of fighting." She paused. "And six new Beasts, if Kensa's spell has worked."

Tom allowed himself a grim smile. "And didn't you hear? Kensa knew who I was. That means she knows we're here to stop her. She'll be cautious, and—"

He broke off, feeling his shield tingle on his back. He held it in front of him. Across the surface from the centre, a red thread like a blood trail led to the left side. Purple light pulsed in the spot where Sepron's tooth had once been embedded. A word appeared: *Elko*.

"It must be the name of the Beast,"

said Elenna. "But what does it have to do with Sepron?"

"Let's find out," said Tom, climbing back onto Tempest. He took a last glance at his shield. Elko's location looked like a ragged coastline rising up to a mountain ridge. Perhaps he was a sea Beast, like the Good Serpent in Avantia. Tom spurred Tempest to a canter then a gallop towards the edge of the plateau. Then the sound of pounding hooves was gone as they took to the air.

Kensa's castle was soon just a smudge on the horizon.

We'll see you again soon, Tom thought, looking back.

CHAPTER SEVEN

CREATURE FROM THE DEEP

The four of them flew over the mountains as the sun crept through Henkrall's sky. They crossed a ridge, and the mountain ranges dropped away. Beyond a wide shelf of land lay the sea, stretching all the way to the horizon. Even with the power of the golden helmet, Tom couldn't see any other land. Rivers like sparkling snakes crossed the wide plain, and Tom swooped low. *We're almost there*, he realised. *But what will we find?*

The rivers gathered into one raging torrent that surged towards the cliff. A rainbow arced through clouds of spray and a distant roaring sound grew louder as they approached.

Tom burst over the edge of the kingdom, above a booming waterfall that cascaded into the ocean.

This is where the shield-map has led us, he thought, *which means a Beast is close*.

He scanned the still water below, but there was no sign of Elko. All he could see were a few floating clumps of what looked like seaweed, bobbing on the surface.

"Perhaps the map's wrong," he called to Elenna.

His friend frowned. "Maybe we should keep our distance, just in case."

Tom gave a grim smile. "You keep an eye out. I'm going closer to take a look."

Tom swooped lower, feeling the wind rush past. Tempest whinnied in delight as his hooves skimmed the water. Tom peered down, but couldn't make anything out. A few seagulls sat happily on the surface, bobbing up and down. They turned and made another pass, but other than a few choppy waves, nothing was out of the ordinary.

Tom thought he heard a shout and looked up. Elenna was waving her arm wildly as she flew closer. "…moving!" he heard her call. "They're moving!"

Tom tugged at Tempest's mane and the flying stallion climbed from the water. Then he saw what Elenna meant. One of the clumps of seaweed seemed to be drifting across the waves.

In fact, they all were. And something else was even odder.

They're moving against the tide!

Tom's heart lurched as he spurred Tempest higher and the seagulls broke into flight with screeching cries. The sea below heaved as weeds collected together and shapes shifted beneath the surface. With an eerie, slithering sound, a hand covered in slimy tendrils rose from the waves. It reached up, fingers stretching to snatch Tom and Tempest from the air. With a burst of speed and a neigh of alarm, the stallion flew clear.

"Good boy, Tempest," Tom muttered, patting the horse's flank as he joined Elenna in the sky.

Elko rose from the water, a giant covered in tangled weeds, slimy fronds and other plants of the sea. Sponges and shellfish clung to his limbs, and Tom made out a skeleton of dark coral beneath. From the depths of his chest a purple heart glowed. Fish fell gasping back into the sea and crabs scuttled from his mouth. The Beast's glowing green eyes settled on Tom, and narrowed to slits.

"He can't reach us here," said Elenna, but Tom could hear the fear in her voice.

Elko walked through the shallows to the base of the giant waterfall, towering nearly as tall. Through the misty spray, the Beast laid a hand

against the rock face. Weeds spilt
from his fingers, crawling over the
rocks and smothering them like living
creatures.

*He'll choke the whole kingdom with
deadly webbing*, thought Tom. *And then*

Avantia too, if Kensa has her way.

Tom drew his sword. His palm was slippery on the hilt as he flew through the mist.

"Be careful!" Elenna called, as she followed on Spark.

Tom flew through the spray towards the ocean menace. With a cry, he hacked at the Beast's wrist, severing his weed-coated hand. It still clutched the cliff-face. Elko turned and laughed, revealing razor-sharp fangs, just like Sepron's. Tom gazed in horror as the weeds from his wrist reached out through the air and tangled themselves with the hand. The fingers flexed again, then swiped at Tom. Tempest ducked beneath the arm, flying close to the cliff-face, then he broke through the mist on the other side.

The wound healed itself before my eyes, Tom thought. *How can I fight a Beast like that?*

"Help me!" called Elenna. Tom steered in the air and saw his friend

hovering above the waterfall. From Elko's outstretched arm a whip of seaweed had lashed itself around Elenna's waist. Tom saw Spark's wings desperately flapping as Elenna fought to stay on his back.

Tom flew towards her, sword raised to hack at the grasping tendril. He saw Elenna's eyes bulging as the breath was squeezed from her lungs. He'd almost reached his friend when Elko tore her loose from Spark and snatched her into the mists below.

"Elenna!" Tom cried, plunging after her into the waterfall's spray.

CHAPTER EIGHT

UNDERWATER BATTLE

The Beast gripped Tom's friend in his fist and her eyes were wide with terror. Spark darted past him, snapping with his jaws at Elko's green, slimy face. The Beast reared back, staggering away from the cliffs with a roar. Tom slashed at the arm holding Elenna, almost cutting through. She screamed as the hand released her, and dropped out of sight into the spray. Next moment, she rose again, lying across Spark's back and clambering into a sitting position. "Good boy!" she shouted, gripping the wolf's furry neck.

Elko spat a mouthful of filthy water into the sea and regained his footing. The wound in his arm magically healed with a thickening growth of sea-plants.

If we can just drive him back where he came from, thought Tom. *We'd have a chance if he was in the sea.*

Elko threw out more ropes of weeds, trying to lasso them, but Tom and Elenna managed to dodge the snaking tendrils.

"Attack from the sides!" Tom called to Elenna. "Go for his legs!"

As Elko lunged towards them, Tom

and Elenna split up and headed in opposite directions. Tom couldn't see exactly where his friend was through the thick mist, but he trusted her to follow their plan. He wheeled round in the air, and drove Tempest towards Elko's knees.

Tom swung his sword, cutting right through the Beast's leg. He saw Elenna, three arrows at her string, shoot all of them at once into the other leg.

Elko rocked as he lost his balance. His huge body leant backwards, one leg completely severed and the other stuck with arrows. New weeds knitted together over the wounds, but it was too late to keep him from toppling. He crashed down into the water, throwing up a giant wave. His body seemed to split into a cloud of weeds.

"Is he dead?" asked Elenna, joining Tom in the sky.

Beneath the surface, Tom saw the weeds clump together once more into the shape of limbs. But Elko didn't burst forth from the water. Instead he swam downwards. He was still very much alive, and Tom knew he had no choice.

"I have to go after him," he said.

He flew low across the water with Elenna at his side. Elko's shape had vanished under the waves.

"You haven't got anything to help you breathe," said Elenna.

Tom scanned the sheer cliffs. On previous Quests, he'd used conch shells to store air, but there was nothing like that here.

"I'll use the Golden Armour's chainmail," he said. "Extra strength of heart will help me hold my breath for longer."

Tom sheathed his sword and kicked off his boots for a better grip. Then he clambered up carefully until he was standing on Tempest's back.

"I'll stay near the water," Elenna said. "You might need some more of my arrows if you can tempt Elko back to the surface."

Tom nodded, took a huge breath, filling his lungs, and leapt off the stallion, angling his body into a steep dive. *I'll either drown or defeat this Beast*, he thought, as he plunged beneath the freezing water. He swam down with powerful strokes until he saw the seabed through the cloudy water. A mass of seaweed carpeted the ocean floor, swaying in the current.

The Beast could be anywhere, Tom thought, expecting a hand to shoot out at any moment. He swam through a shoal of tiny silver fish, like glittering coins. Their fins tickled his ears, his ribs, then his legs.

A strange creaking groan sounded through the water as if somewhere the hull of a ship was running aground. The seaweed pulsed with a dim purple light and a sharp pain on Tom's cheek made him gasp. Then there was a sting on his wrist. The fish were darting at his body, nipping him, then retreating. One of the tiny fish sank its teeth into his ankle and Tom shook it loose. He tried desperately not to panic. *I've got to save air*, he thought.

As the shoal continued to swirl and gnash around him, Tom drew his sword and cut arcs to scatter them. He managed to strike a few, leaving trails of blood in the water. The injured fish broke away and the rest fled too.

Tom's lungs were starting to burn. Where was the Beast?

More shapes drifted a short distance away – bigger fish attracted by the bubbles and the scent of blood. Tom recognised the sleek profile of a shark, its nose like a blunt blade pressing towards him. More followed, cutting through the depths.

I can't fight the Beast and *a shoal of sharks!*

The first shark darted at him, its eyes rolling back in its head. Tom smashed his sword hilt into the creature's nose and sent it reeling. But the others came on, from every side. Tom realised he was bleeding from several of the fish bites, so more

sharks would come. Elko would have to wait.

He kicked upwards, peering down to see the sharks in pursuit. Their powerful tails drove them through the water, and their mouths split into grins of jagged teeth. The light above grew stronger as he heaved himself towards the surface. But the sharks were gaining, and Tom waited to feel their teeth slice into his flesh.

CHAPTER NINE

WAKING THE BEAST

Tom broke the surface, taking in great gasps of air. The first thing he saw was Tempest, hooves dipping in the water as he hovered. Tom reached up and threw an arm around Tempest's neck as the horse sank closer to the water, bending at the knees. A shark lunged, snapping with its jaws.

An arrow thudded into the shark's flank, sending it crashing back

into the water.

"Thank you!" Tom gasped, clambering up onto Tempest's back.

"What happened?" Elenna asked. "You're injured!"

Now Tom saw it wasn't only a few bites. His clothes were stained all over with patches of blood, his skin covered with tiny stinging cuts where the fish had attacked him. He told Elenna what had happened. "I have to go back down," he said.

"You can't!" Elenna cried. "The fish will attack you again."

And that will bring more sharks… Tom thought.

"Elko must have a weakness," said Tom. "Kensa's controlling him somehow."

He thought back to when he'd faced his first sea Beast – Sepron. The Sea Serpent had been enchanted by a collar placed around his neck by Malvel. But Elko had no collar.

"Think!" said Elenna. "Was there anything unusual about Elko?"

Tom frowned. The fish had seemed friendly at first, but they'd turned nasty when he heard the odd noise and…

"The seaweed changed colour!" he said. "It turned purple, just like Elko's heart. That's when the fish attacked me."

"The Beast must have been controlling them," said Elenna.

"Then maybe I can do the same," said Tom, fingering the purple jewel in his belt. "Perhaps this will help." The sun's rays broke through the clouds of mist in glowing shards of light.

He jumped off Tempest's back again, landing with a splash. Treading water, he undid his belt, holding it taut between his fists. When Tom angled the belt in the water, the jewels caught the sunlight and threw off spokes of rainbow light.

Soon, shoals of fish started to gather around him.

Tom eyed the fish, trying not to panic. If they all turned and attacked at once, he'd be eaten alive!

But the fish remained where they were and his heartbeat slowed. They bobbed in the water, all pointing towards him.

"It's working!" Elenna said, watching from above.

It's almost as if they're waiting for instructions, he thought.

He slowly refastened his belt, took another deep breath and dipped his head beneath the waves. As one, copying his movement, the fish turned to swim down too. *They obey the person with a purple light!* Tom struck out towards the seabed, until he saw the same mass of weed as before. He pointed towards it and the fish shot past him, straight at the ocean floor.

The shoals buried themselves in the weeds, darting in and out and creating clouds of sand. Tom heard a roar that shook the water around him, and the purple glow spread across the writhing tendrils. Crabs and tiny squid burst from their hiding places. *Found you!* Tom thought. The fish had helped to uncover Elko's hiding place.

The Beast began to take shape ahead of him, seeming to grow right out of the seabed. Weeds tangled and gathered into knots as the Beast's frame rose up. The giant head of Elko was facing away from him, so Tom kicked forward and gripped one of the massive slimy arms.

Water rushed through Tom's hair and clothes as Elko straightened up, up, up, dragging Tom after him. He was torn from the water and lifted high over the waves.

He felt his hands slipping on the dangling weeds and his heart lurched. If he fell from this height, he'd probably break his neck when he hit the water. Gritting his teeth, he wrapped his legs around more of the seaweed and crossed his ankles for extra support. Elko lurched around wildly, roaring in anger, and Tom saw Elenna high above on Spark, levelling an arrow at their foe.

Together we can defeat this Beast, Tom thought.

Elko thrashed as Elenna's arrow lodged in his neck, and Tom clung on to the underside of his arm. At any

moment, it felt like he'd be thrown
off into the water far below. Saltwater
flecked his eyes, making him blink, but
through the blur he saw the Beast's
purple heart glowing in his chest.

*Could that be the secret to the
enchantment?* Tom thought.

But he'd have to get to it first. Tom released his grip with one hand and reached further up Elko's arm, seizing another fistful of weed. He kept his legs locked tight and made his way slowly along the arm towards Elko's shoulder. The Beast was still focused on Elenna. Keeping below Elko's line of sight, Tom reached for the Beast's chest. He was nearly there – he could feel the sweat trickling down his spine. *If I can just...*

A wild snorting made Tom's head snap around. He jerked back as a chain whip thumped across the Beast's chest.

Elko roared in pain and Tom saw Igor swoop past on his hog.

"Missed!" the hunchback said with a cackle. "You're about to die, Avantian!"

CHAPTER TEN

DOUBLE JEOPARDY

Igor turned his hog deftly in the air, swinging his whip over his head.

"Keep him back!" Tom yelled to Elenna.

His friend was already pulling her bowstring as she climbed from behind Elko. Tom saw Igor's eye widen and he tugged on his hog's bristles. The arrow streaked past, grazing the creature's underbelly. With a snort, the hog

veered wildly to one side and Igor had
to cling to its neck with both hands.

That should keep him busy for a while,
Tom thought. *Now I've got a job to do…*

He continued to climb the side of
Elko's slippery chest. From time to
time he glimpsed the Beast's coral
skeleton beneath the thick hide of
weeds. He was getting closer to the
purple glowing heart. Elko's lips
parted in a roar of defiance as he
spotted Tom, and his fingers reached
to grasp him. Tom let go just in time
and leapt sideways, then grabbed
onto a string of tangled fronds under
the Beast's armpit. Breathing hard,
he passed around to the Beast's
back, climbing hand over hand. Elko
grunted and twisted, snatching at the
air wildly. But Tom had reached a
spot right in the centre of the Beast's

back where Elko couldn't reach.

What now? Tom asked himself. *I'm the wrong side of the Beast to attack the heart!*

Elko stopped trying to grab Tom and surged through the water, back towards the plunging waterfall. Tom realised his plan. *He wants to wash me off!*

He quickly unfastened his belt with one hand and lashed it against Elko's shoulder. The Beast bellowed as the buckle tangled in the foliage of his skin, latching on like a grappling hook.

"Hang on!" yelled Elenna.

They passed into the falls and Tom's ears were filled with the thunder of water. It pummelled him like a hundred fists, and he clung on grimly.

Through the cascade, Tom saw a cave beyond, its roof covered in dripping stalactites like dangling dagger blades, and its floor jutting with stalagmites. They gave him an idea, but he'd need Elenna's help. And Igor's.

"Elenna!" he shouted. "Fly into the waterfall!"

There was no way to know if she'd heard him, and he wasn't sure how much longer he could hang on in the relentless onslaught of water. Elko was turning and jerking, pulling his body in and out of the waterfall in an effort to shake Tom loose.

"Hurry!" Tom called.

Suddenly two shapes shot through

the mist, level with the Beast's waist.
Elenna! And... Igor was right on her
tail, his whip dangling. *Just a bit
closer...* Tom thought.

Igor drew back his arm, ready to
deliver a blow.

"Duck!" Tom shouted to his friend.

Elenna weaved to one side and
down as Igor lashed out. The chains
missed Elenna and Spark, and
thumped into the top of the Beast's
leg. Elko's roars shook the cavern
as the Beast staggered among the
stalagmites. He tripped, his arms
wheeling for balance, then he began
to tip over. Tom hung on as the
massive Beast toppled. Elko's body
cushioned his fall, but Tom rolled off,
winded and dizzy.

The Beast's cries died in an instant.
As Tom struggled to his feet he saw

why. A stalagmite had punched a
hole right through the middle of
Elko's body, and on its tip rested
the purple heart.

The Lord of the Sea quivered and
the weeds began to shrivel across his
whole form. The green light of his eyes
dimmed as he melted into a mass of
stinking seaweed over the cave floor.

"No!" shouted Igor, hovering above

Tom. "It can't be!"

Tom climbed to his feet and drew his sword. "Go back to Kensa!" he said. "Tell her that you've killed her Beast yourself!"

Igor's face paled. "We'll meet again!" he yelled, then plunged back through the waterfall.

Elenna flew down towards Tom, and he saw Tempest flying at her side. The horse alighted on the rocks and ruffled his wings. Tom climbed on, and directed the brave stallion towards the stalagmite that had killed the Beast. The heart had shrunk to a beautiful purple jewel as big as his fist. Tom plucked it off and tucked it into his tunic.

"Let's go and dry off," he called to Elenna. Tired and soaking, they broke through the waterfall again and climbed back to the cliff top overlooking the vast ocean. Dismounting, Tom patted Tempest on his damp neck. The stallion's flanks were heaving with exhaustion. "I owe you a big thank you," he said.

"They've certainly proved their loyalty," said Elenna, as Spark shook a shower of water droplets from his fur.

Tom and Elenna sat side by side, letting the sun dry the clothes on their backs. Tom looked back across the strange new kingdom. There were five more Beasts to face. *And if each is as deadly as Elko...*

Tom felt his shield vibrate. Was it already showing the next Beast? He took it off his back, and saw one of the empty spaces glowing purple.

"Perhaps..." Elenna began.

Tom reached inside his tunic for the

purple jewel. As he drew it out, he gasped. His hand didn't hold a jewel at all. He'd pulled out Sepron's tooth! "It's transformed!" he said, slotting the token into his rightful home.

"Maybe we'll get all the tokens back if we defeat the six Beasts of Henkrall," said Elenna.

"*When* we defeat them," Tom said. Though the Golden Armour was stored safely in the Palace in Avantia, in that moment he sensed it on his shoulders, solid and reassuring. He thought of his father, resting in the Gallery of Tombs, and felt a rush of pride. All kingdoms needed someone to stand up for them, including Henkrall. This was a burden he was happy to bear.

"While there's blood in my veins," he said, "Kensa will never triumph."

Join Tom on the next stage
of the Beast Quest when he meets

Tarrok
THE BLOOD SPIKE

Win an exclusive
Beast Quest T-shirt and goody bag!

In every Beast Quest book the Beast Quest logo is
hidden in one of the pictures. Find the logos in books
61 to 66 and make a note of which pages they appear
on. Write the six page numbers on a postcard and
send it in to us.
Each month we will draw one winner to receive
a Beast Quest T-shirt and goody bag.

THE BEAST QUEST COMPETITION:
THE NEW AGE
Orchard Books
338 Euston Road, London NW1 3BH
Australian readers should email:
childrens.books@hachette.com.au

New Zealand readers should write to:
Beast Quest Competition
4 Whetu Place, Mairangi Bay, Auckland, NZ
or email: childrensbooks@hachette.co.nz

Only one entry per child.
Final draw: 2 September 2013

You can also enter this competition
via the Beast Quest website: www.beastquest.co.uk

Join the Quest,
Join the Tribe

www.beastquest.co.uk

Have you checked out the Beast Quest website?
It's the place to go for games, downloads, activities,
sneak previews and lots of fun!

You can read all about your favourite Beasts,
download free screensavers and desktop wallpapers
for your computer, and even challenge your friends
to a Beast Tournament.

Sign up to the newsletter at www.beastquest.co.uk
to receive exclusive extra content and the
opportunity to enter special members-only
competitions. We'll send you up-to-date info on all
the Beast Quest books, including the next exciting
series which features six brand-new Beasts!

Get 30% off all Beast Quest Books at www.beastquest.co.uk
Enter the code BEAST at the checkout.

All books priced at £4.99.
Special bumper editions priced at £5.99.

Orchard Books are available from all good bookshops, or can be ordered from our website: www.orchardbooks.co.uk, or telephone 01235 827702, or fax 01235 8227703.

 Beast Quest®

Series 11: THE NEW AGE
COLLECT THEM ALL!

A new land, a deadly enemy and six new Beasts
await Tom on his next adventure!

978 1 40831 841 6

978 1 40831 842 3

978 1 40831 843 0

978 1 40831 844 7

978 1 40831 845 4

978 1 40831 846 1

Series 12: THE DARKEST HOUR
Out January 2013

Meet six terrifying new Beasts!

Solak Scourge of the Sea
Kajin the Beast Catcher
Issrilla the Creeping Menace
Vigrash the Clawed Eagle
Mirka the Ice Horse
Kama the Faceless Beast

Watch out for the next Special Bumper Edition
OUT MARCH 2013!

OUT NOW!

MEET A NEW HERO OF AVANTIA

ISBN: 978 1 408 31867 6

Danger stirs in the land of Avantia.

Maximus, son of Evil Wizard Malvel, has stolen the
magical Golden Gauntlet. Using its power he plans
to force the Good Beasts, Ferno and Epos,
to fight each other to the death!

The Chronicles of Avantia

FROM THE DARK, A HERO ARISES...

Dare to enter the kingdom of Avantia.

A new evil arises in Avantia. Lord Derthsin has ordered his armies into the four corners of Avantia. If the four Beasts of Avantia can find their Chosen Riders they might have the strength to challenge Derthsin. But if they fail, the land of Avantia will be lost forever...

FIRST HERO, CHASING EVIL, CALL TO WAR, FIRE AND FURY- OUT NOW!

www.chroniclesofavantia.com

NEW ADAM BLADE SERIES

Coming soon 2013

Robobeasts battle in this deep sea cyber adventure.

Read on for an exclusive extract of
CEPHALOX THE CYBERSQUID!

The Merryn's Touch

The water was up to Max's knees and still rising. Soon it would reach his waist. Then his chest. Then his face.

I'm going to die down here, he thought.

He hammered on the dome with all his strength, but the plexiglass held firm.

Then he saw something pale looming through the dark water outside the submersible. A long, silvery spike. It must be the squid-creature, with one of its weird robotic attachments. Any second now it would smash the glass and finish him off...

There was a crash. The sub rocked. The silver spike thrust through the broken plexiglass. More water surged in. Then the spike withdrew and the water poured in faster. Max forced his way against the torrent to the opening. If he could just squeeze through the gap...

The pressure pushed him back. He took one last deep breath, and then the water was

over his head.

He clamped his mouth shut. He struggled forwards, feeling the pressure in his lungs build.

Something gripped his arms, but it wasn't the squid's tentacle – it was a pair of hands, pulling him through the hole. The broken plexiglass scraped his sides – and then he was through.

The monster was nowhere to be seen. In the dim underwater light, he made out the face of his rescuer. It was the Merryn girl, and next to her was a large silver swordfish.

She smiled at him.

Max couldn't smile back. He'd been saved from a metal coffin, only to swap it for a watery one. The pressure of the ocean squeezed him on every side. His lungs felt as though they were bursting.

He thrashed his limbs, rising upwards.

He looked to where he thought the surface was, but saw nothing, only endless water. His cheeks puffed with the effort to hold in air. He let some of it out slowly, but it only made him want to breathe in more.

He knew he had no chance. He was too deep, he'd never make it to the surface. Soon he'd no longer be able to hold his breath. The water would swirl into his lungs and he'd die here, at the bottom of the sea. *Just like my mother*, he thought.

The Merryn girl rose up beside him, reached out and put her hands on his neck. Warmth seemed to flow from her fingers. Then the warmth turned to pain. What was happening? It got worse and worse, until he felt as if his throat was being ripped open. Was she trying to kill him?

He struggled in panic, trying to push her off. His mouth opened and water rushed in.

That was it. He was going to die.

Then he realised something – the water was cool and sweet. He sucked it down into his lungs. Nothing had ever tasted so good.

He was breathing underwater!

He put his hands to his neck and found two soft, gill-like openings where the Merryn

girl had touched him. His eyes widened in astonishment.

The girl smiled.

There was something else strange. Max found he could see more clearly. The water seemed lighter and thinner. He made out the shapes of underwater plants, rock formations and shoals of fish in the distance, which had been invisible before. And he didn't feel as if the ocean was crushing him any more.

Is this what it's like to be a Merryn? he wondered.

"I'm Lia," said the girl. "And this is Spike." She patted the swordfish on the back and it nuzzled against her.

"Hi, I'm Max." He clapped his hand to his mouth in shock. He was speaking the same strange language of sighs and whistles he'd heard the girl use when he first met her –

but now it made sense, as if he was born to speak it.

"What have you done to me?"

"Saved your life," said Lia. "You're welcome, by the way."

"Oh – don't think I'm not grateful – I am. But – you've turned me into a Merryn?"

The girl laughed. "Not exactly – but I've given you some Merryn powers. You can breath underwater, speak our language, and your senses are much stronger. Come on – we need to get away from here. The Cybersquid may come back."

In one graceful movement she slipped onto Spike's back. Max clambered on behind her.

"Hold tight," Lia said. "Spike – let's go!"

Max put his arms around the Merryn's waist. He was jerked backwards as the swordfish shot off through the water, but he managed to hold on.

They raced above underwater forests of gently waving fronds, and hills and valleys of rock. Max saw giant crabs scuttling over the seabed. Undersea creatures loomed up – jellyfish, an octopus, a school of dolphins – but Spike nimbly swerved round them.

"Where are we going?" Max asked.

"You'll see," Lia said over her shoulder.

"I need to find my dad," Max said. The crazy things that had happened in the last few moments had driven his father from his mind. Now it all came flooding back. Was his dad gone for good? "We have to do something! That monster's got my dad – and my dogbot too!"

"It's not the squid who wants your father. It's the Professor who's *controlling* the squid. I tried to warn you back at the city – but you wouldn't listen."

"I didn't understand you then!"

"You Breathers don't try to understand – that's your whole problem!"

"I'm trying now. What is that monster? And who is the Professor?"

"I'll explain everything when we arrive."

"Arrive where?"

The seabed suddenly fell away. A steep valley sloped down, leading way, way deeper than the ocean ridge Aquora was built on. The swordfish dived. The water grew darker.

Far below, Max saw a faint yellow glimmer. As he watched it grew bigger and brighter, until it became a vast undersea city of golden-glinting rock rushing up towards them. There were towers, spires, domes, bridges, courtyards, squares, gardens. A city as big as Aquora, and far more beautiful, at the bottom of the sea.

Max gasped in amazement. The water was dark, but the city emitted a glow of its own

– a warm phosphorescent light that spilled
from the many windows. The rock sparkled.
Orange, pink and scarlet corals and seashells
decorated the walls in intricate patterns.

"This is – amazing!" he said.

Lia turned round and smiled at him. "It's our home," she said. "Sumara!"

Calling all Adam Blade fans!
We need YOU!

Are you a huge fan of Beast Quest? Is Adam Blade your favourite author? Do you want to know more about his new series, Sea Quest, before anybody else IN THE WORLD?

We're looking for 100 of the most loyal Adam Blade fans to become Sea Quest Cadets.

So how do I become a Sea Quest Cadet?

Simply go to **www.seaquestbooks.co.uk** and fill in the form.

What do I get if I become a Sea Quest Cadet?

You will be one of a limited number of people to receive exclusive Sea Quest merchandise.

What do I have to do as a Sea Quest Cadet?
Take part in Sea Quest activities with your friends!

ENROL TODAY!
SEA QUEST NEEDS YOU!

Open to UK and Republic of Ireland residents only.